The Woe of R

GW01417920

Mathew Horto

Part 1

Book 1
The Ballad of Agnes Bean

Book 2
The Chronicle of Thomas Hume

Book 3
The Tale of the Ruined Hume and Bean

Part 2

Book 4
Dimmock's Yellow Diary

Book 5
Matwau Rising

Part 3

Book 6
The Fears of Eleanor Dare

Book 7
Wahunsonacock

Epilogue

Part 1

Book 1
The Ballad of Agnes Bean

Narrator-
It wasn't the gale that chilled his skin
As he mulled on the cannibal captured
within.
In trembling state he clenched his cane
To rap on the gate of the jail in the rain.

The jailer bade enter, unbolted the door
And jolted the ragged convict on the floor.
He shook himself down to render some warm
Then span in alarm as she seized his arm.

Agnes-

"Close to me, notary!
Sit near if you dare.
Sunrise I'll swing from my tree of the hair.
Wring your wet cloak and I'll narrate
The tale of the thousand folks that was ate."

"Put quill to ink and I will tell
Of those that now burn in hell.
I'll tell of my past, that place I abhor
And them that scared Scotland
For years five and score."

"They say I'm a witch
Which I say to them nay!
I'm a Christian now,
I know how to pray.
I'm repented of sin, lamented the crime.
A new sons arrived. A husband who's kind.
And my slate to lave this last night I'm
confined.
But your words just might leave my men
unmolested
For I am the last of the Beans arrested…"

"He's your boy!"
"It's a brute"

"He's a Bean!"
"It's a mute"
"Och hold your son, Father, for he is no freak"
"That it is blinkered wife,
 It's got whiskers and teeth!"
"He's smiling!"
"That's scowling. And why's it not howling?
I swear it by god it's laying there growling!
And hold it I'll not. In its pit eyes I've seen
That predators stare. I swear it's no Bean.
But a wolf clothed in a babes pink skin.
Imps have taken my innocent kin!
And swapped it with this…
A goblin twin!"

"He tore at the breast, saw jest in the wail
And so was suckled straight from a pail.
He came into the world callous and brawny
Alexander she named him.
They nicknamed him Sawney."

"He was kept in a pen most day and all night
'Cause for he could walk he would crawl for a fight.
He bit all his brothers and strangled his pets

And snarled at his parents
And dismissed their threats."

"At night with the family fearful in bed
The yearling would laugh as he filled them
with dread.
He'd bark and howl as he smashed up his
room
And chillingly bout with himself in the
gloom."

"His pa was crofting away in Killwinning
When Sawney, aged 7, wet his taste with a
killing.
He was grabbed in the fields by the twins
McTavish
Who trussed him in twin to beat him savage.
'You ugly Ned. Trespass you dare!
We'll bat your head and burn your hair
We'll break your arms, ten fingers and then
We'll beat you up for burning our den."

"The teens took turns to sear him with brands
From the fire he'd lit in McTavish's lands.
He roared through the pain, the smell and the
smoke

Then tolled their knell when he gnawed the rope."

"His Pa had tried to teach him his trade
But Sawney the youth had only displayed
An utter contempt for manual work
And daily slunk off to rob from the kirk."

"An encounter at twelve whilst digging a ditch
Was a vicious tryst with a fiery bitch
Who smashed her fists into Sawney Bean
When taunted with smut
She deemed obscene"

'Fight like a man! You bit me, you swine!'

'Off me big wench. I'll snapeth your spine'

"He tore at her clothes
She flattened his nose.
And gouged his eyes
And yanked his hair.
A counter attack laid bosoms bare.
Then bloodied and ripped he mounted the mare.

And then they were hitched.
Pa and the bitch.
She showed him tricks to make them rich.
She was his match in harsh and vice
And the pair of them both were the flip side
of nice."

"Before he had anger. With her came rage.
They planned to fly, escape the cage
Of labouring life in his ancestral home.
Fools had gold they'd claim their own."

"Flew the nest in early teens.
Trade was made by menacing means.
They found their way through the threat of a
flay.
Folks in fear for their lives would pay."

"Gert would flirt with drunks in the Inn.
Her trunked thighs seemed slim with gin.
She'd flounce them out with a kiss and a
grope.
Pa would pounce, his dirk to their throat."

'Now it's awakened! No. You'll not runaway.
Come to me lass. For a roll in the hay.'

"By her hair he hauled her, this horny goat herder
Sawney in wait saw his third gory murder.
Now wanted for trial the pair of them fled.
Night times through towns hunting for bread
To the forest of Galloway, there to make camp
To give birth to the first in then cold and the damp."

"Address you your notes,
Nervous young clerk!
I was pressed out to the dark!
Five years in a pit with a fern for a door
A tool for food in the soil on the floor.
Rat and root and dreams of boar."

"Winter and wolves and snow on the ground
Saw sisters of mine buried under a mound.
Hunger pangs stabbed all us three.
Worse was the wail of the spirit banshee."

"Mother – curse her! Felt 'em inside her
When pa, in the den, heard the sound of a rider.

Sprang out he with stealth and bought to the
floor
A pitiful father of a family of four.

Not even a coin had the man when he died
By his groin dragged into our hide.
With famines thin fingers clawing within
He made us a meal from his first severed
limb."

"I sat and I watched and I ate and I learned.
By the glint in their eyes I saw that they'd
turned.
With blood spattered chins I saw it first then.
Addicts! That thirst for flesh of me!"

"The meat made ma strong and after she bore
A triplet of boys. Then there came more.
Scores of poor riders died every year
'Till none ventured in to the forest of fear."

"Our home was a hall from the bones of the
mauled
With us now numbering ten.
Logan's laird for Reevers came
Through the woodland with all of his men."

"We scattered before the hand of the law
Rumbled our slaughter house midden.
Sawney I saw by Satan was driven
To the coast and a cavern near to Girvan."

"A serpentine tunnel, fathoms deep
Became his castle and our keep.
Out from this fume filled torchlit lair
He'd venture forth to plundered snare.
Those alone and sometimes pairs."

"From a child I grew and I witnessed lots
My toys were robbed off of eaten Scots.
My clothes the finest clothing stolen.
From wretched souls our bellies swollen."

"I alone he'd take to fairs
Our pockets wide with others wares.
There we'd stock with things we need.
He'd get blind drunk on honey mead,
Tell of his past and twisted creed."

"A starving start saw me late to bloom.
Fresh man flesh flowered five to groom.
He most needed mead supplies

And I could calm suspicious eyes."

"So I was special just to him
A small respite for it was grim.
An appetite unsatiated, eased a bit inebriated
Elspeth was the first pregnated.
Megan next then vexed Fannie
Dwarfish Elsie, cyclops Annie…"

"Half his army was his harem.
Hefty as the males and wild.
Bullied me to urchin minding,
I, the eldest, looked a child"

"Mother said-
'You'll ne'r produce!'
And started a chronic abuse."

"The Bean boys voices all got deep,
Bullocks bodies, minds of sheep.
With a band of bambinos to keep
Larger groups attacked and taken.
His cravings never seemed to slacken."

"In the cave I stayed! Kept far from danger.
I never went. Never killed a stranger!

Never allowed out on a raid
But stayed and worked a nursery maid.
Ma stayed too, a wet nursed turned
And I was beat and I was burned."

"But once a month and sometimes more
I'd leave the lair and there I saw
In Girvan town where folk where trading
Livings earned not got through raiding.
Good men, children, none deformed!
In secret thought 'I'll be reformed!
And do what's right and not grow old
A troglodyte! Doing what she's told."

"When the one eyed one birthed twenty two
Mother sat and refused to move.
Motionless in morbid rest,
Queues of bairns to her baggy breast.
For me she'd only rise, to batter.
The milkmaid sat and just got fatter."

"So many moons I tended brats and mended
wounds.
I skinned and dried the lifeless hides
And racked them in our store.
Mother did no chore because

She weighed the same as four."

"Able cadavers I would salt,
Boiling all those scrawny.
Stewed the parts to feed the clan
The heart was kept for Sawney."

"His idle state would slump away
When he ate the pump then he would bay
'I'll fight all eight!'
And then he'd wrestle
Massive sons gorged on gristle
And always win for Sawney Bean
Full of heart was thrice as mean!"

"Twas all the worse when the tide was high
Buried under ground. Away from the sky
Black and dank, with the mead drank dry.
Hiding blind amongst bairns for I had no bust
But I sensed his rage and I smelt his lust."

"We'd an unseen hole where the sea came to swirl
Where none could fit but a waif.
In the dark echoed groans, screams and moans

We shivered there wet but safe."

"When my chest at last did grow
I was whipped as fathers beau.
The suckling sow sliced into me!
Cruel with insane jealousy!"

"You!
 With that nauseous look upon your face
For the things I tell of my disgrace!
I was raised a slave in a vampires cave!
But I swear my souls been saved!
And I was but coal till he made me whole
So pen your scroll and don't shake with fright
For the things I tell on this stormy night
'Twas all before I saw Gods shining light."

"I'd never a friend save one carrion crow
Who came every day to be fed
Eye to eye it seemed to know
My depths of despair and dread."

"My abhorrent parent bent my mind!
I sought suicide and almost died.
I swam to the crag and nearly drowned,
Ran to the moor. I was always found

And then I was enraptured."

"In my dark despair shone a shaft of light
One autumn night, I was struck first sight
Then I cherished life when live Englishmen
were captured."

"Blue bloods, five, only half alive
And sixteen year old Timothy Demure.
Linked by chain and a world of pain
I cried in shame to think what he'd endure."

"They shuffled in, beaten men
And all had a dreadful pallor.
But by the wounds of the tribe
And Sawney's vibe
They must have fought with valour."

"His wrath was high for he'd lost an eye
And he grabbed me by my mane
'My tone is low so you will go
And bring me the heart of the Thane!"

"But the Thane he fought
When I sought his heart
For never a live one did.

And the triplets came to butcher the Thane
And Timothy I hid."

"Another night ambush he had planned
For in winter time was harder.
Ordered out his band under strict command
To stock high our sordid larder."

"Thus hid from the horde he spoke as a Lord
An accent I'd trouble translating.
But he made it clear, he was such a dear.
My fore fear was she who sat lactating."

"If father was a riot on his organ diet
Then brains as a mains the reverse.
None the sharpest flint.
Not one had a hint.
As food for thought they were worse."

"So he lay undiscovered
In the nest of the buzzard
My crush completely sealed.
And I tried not to show my innermost glow
Or reveal my angel concealed."

"The aristocrat hicks got eat in weeks.

When I felt his horror surge
I'd urge him peak by my nimble cheeks
Then I'd serenade him with a dirge."

"Neath a curtain of arms I ground my charms
Covert behind a wall of skulls.
When he would pall for an anguished bawl
I'd tell him the sounds were gulls."

"Till the shortest day I'd force a lay,
Pinned with a shackled leather tether.
Till the longest night and a promise of flight
When we'd both elope together."

"On the equinox morning I awoke with a
warning
That something was amiss.
Up slithered mother with a breakfast
undercover
And shattered my happiness bliss."

"Oh Agnes I've been wrong!
Eat this. Go on!
Better as a mother I'll get!"

"A crocodile hug, offed the quadruped slug.

I broke the fast and then a sweat."

"With deep suspicion for her kindly mission,
A distrust of her most changed ilk.
I followed a smear as I'd lost my fear
Of a spiral of blood and milk."

"It bled to the head made fence.
I spied the open shackle, heard her broken cackle
My dire came back intense.
The hideous trail of the vast female
Thence went to her snug.
And smothered in a rug with her round face smug
Sat the leathered mound of she.
I uncovered the sheet.
There clamped to her teet
Was the head of Timothy."

"My grief was stunning. Tears were running
I snatched six foot of yew.
Dazed I raised the wood with which
I'd smash the fat bitch in two."

"Fazed for a second then mother beckoned

With a laugh to lower the staff.
With my yearning burned
I froze when I turned…
For Sawney Bean had returned."

"The heart! His heart! She's ate your part!
She's drained your casks!
She claims divinity!
She's hid a lover undercover
And she's made her mother suffer
The brunt so viscously!"

"For my life I did grovel
In the crab covered offal.
Crouched in painful cringe.
He raised his cane then thought again
For he'd got no Hogmanay binge."

"Heretic!
The clan were fuming. Throwing stones
And then exhuming Timmy's limbs
And throwing them. My face a bruise
And full of phlegm.
Death was looming, Sawney then
Bade them stop and hailed for silence
Stopped the stoning and the violence."

"Be still my flock! I've one last mission!
Before you rock it to perdition.
I'll make you come, blasphemous runt
To booze to buy and be my front!"

"Riding beside him, my neck in his claw
Sheer terror was striking but all the folk saw.
Was a dad loading festive fare for a caper.
My mouth said nought but my eyes cried -
'Murder!!'"

"Cuffed to the cart from Girvan town
A dagger wrapped inside my gown
While Sawney whistled tunes at leisure
Contented with fermented pleasure.
For he had siphoned off a barrel
My whole rang with predicted peril."

"With glassy eye the nasty lech
Eased his paw from off my neck."

"A favour! Then I'll set you free.
Sit! Teasing whore, upon my knee."

"By the fire in his eye

And his quick rank breath
I saw the lie. Saw rape saw death.
Sawney saw his double vim.
My heart and the heart of Tim."

"He plied himself, decanting liquor
Untied my bond, his panting quicker.
He reached out for my hair to stroke
I skewered his hand into the oak!
And jumped and ran the speed of wind
And yet he pumped, to drink was pinned."

"Camouflaged in a meadow
I heard him bellow, till the morrow
Then spur his ass.
But on I lay through night and day
Till my bones were froze in the grass."

"In the field I was found
By ploughman Brown
And the simpleton I've since wed.
I've been a good wife.
This sons my life!
But a tear for Tim is still shed!"

"Ten years past my past hit hard

So I went and found a saviour.
I sought retribution and was given absolution
By a priest, for a sexual favour."

Book 2
The Chronicle of Thomas Hume

Narrator-
The solemn scribe, sore Thomas Hume
Stood slow and strode the room.
A thunderous crack didn't change his tack
And his face was a mask of doom.

Thomas-
"Ten whole years! Five hundred men!
That dismal decade should've ended then!
Think of all those lives not saved
When you were not the vampires slave!"

"Innocent play upon the shore
With friends abound and then no more.
Because of grizzled finds of gore.
Then my boyhood shrivelled and ceased

When I was shielded from the beast."

"In solitary isolation.
No playmate to grace my station.
A little hell, hotel Stranraer!
Sick at night from all the fear!
Stiff with fright for year 'pon year.
What other suffers might it bring?
This spectral wicked winged thing."

"But what was worse was my seclusion,
Worse than all demon delusion.
Lonely. Only hotel guests
Would spare a word before their quests.
It came to this - I'd face the fate!
If I could just play with a mate."

"One nightmare night when I fourteen
I woke to find a nightmare scene.
The sky was bright from flame of torch
And piercing it was spear and fork."

"The sheriff with a punk band baying
Accused my father of the slaying.
Told him of the evidence.
Then built a gallows from our fence."

"We had board six English types.
One a Lord and four were Knights.
And the dandies from the south
Had signed the hotel log book out."

"I screamed to Jesus 'Pray it stop!'
-The hangman was a man of frock.
The noose was tightened by the parson.
A forced recluse, now half an orphan."

"I held his feet so he could save
A final word before his grave…

'Thomas Hume, I've groomed thee strong
So go my son and right the wrong.
Seek you the truth and with the proof
Proclaim our name with pride again."

"So I'm not scared!
And my nerves are not frayed!
The emotion is hate! That's been displayed
And I'll pity you not, foul Agnes the black
For you could have told to turn the tide
back."

"Ostracised! And while we mourned
Panes were broke and paint adorned .
Mother scorned, as other owners
Of taverns who had hosted rovers.
The landlord of the inn at Ayr
Hung as hikers last seen there.
The publican of the pub 'The Bear'
Lynched by just a signature."

"And many more, their loved ones too
Grieving when the mob charged through.
Any hamlet near and where
Bones were washed up from the mer."

"A reject in her own commune
Mother saw no oppurtune
A lunacy saw naked stray
She off the cliff at Moroch bay."

"Necessity uplifted me!
I sold the abode and I hitched on carts
To Edinburgh and education.
I wrote reports on the renegade courts
And of the missing gripping the nation."

"My psyche was scarred. Street life was hard

So I turned a bard for my bread.
Reams I filled with the streams of killed.
I wrote in a broad sheet spread"

"I wrote in verse for prose was worse,
The crimes in rhymes were shorter.
The Edinburgh Times bought up my work
Then employed me a court reporter."

"My odes on the rogues soon ran to the road
Of regal recognition.
All the travesty inked I was goad to be linked
To his majesty and audition."

"I entered his chamber the wordsmith painter.
A favoured Makar macabre.
In his innermost ring I had swung the swing
To a patronage from a pauper."

"I feigned effete for the Royal seat
To list all lives been lifted.
Although my work now obsolete
I penned the deceit of the twisted."

"Heed priests whore! Desist your wail!
Shut up your awful yelling!

It is almost dawn and as last of the spawn
You'll listen, for there's more needs telling.
'Tis of your kin that I'm steeped in sin,
I played the gay laureate
'Twas pride for my name
That I suffered the shame
And rode the Kings wicked chariot!"

"So in Scotland's west still more arrests
In the hamlets, towns and shanties.
And the people fled or stayed in dread
Of the ghoul or the vigilantes."

"Tracks went sparse from mass clearance
In reaction to the slaughter.
And on it went, the disappearance
With scores rent off every quarter."

"And all the prayers in all the kirks
And all the pens from all the clerks
Writing up such vast rewards
And fighting men with sharpened swords
In mustered crews, try they might
Could not flush the phantom blight."

"A chain of plays I thus obtained

From the tide of pain in the tyrants reign.
'Till a fortune shift in a winters mist.
Love slain in fey terrain."

'Stop calling me Belle!' Pleaded Claire
She said as she sat on her Colt from the fair

'Please stop else after we're wed
That silly name I'll be known instead'
Said captain Enn of the foot regiment
'Your beauty it doth make my heart
resonant.'
She reached to touch him
'Ride close to me'
As a cloaking fog rolled from the sea."

"Out from the silent smokey white
A violent croak that put to flight
Her mount. And then a pack of beasts
Materialised with screams

 'BEAN FEASTS!"

"A horde of forty freaks came roaring
Swarmed then struck and then got goring
The horse that had sat Claire astride

And killed the Colt and the would be bride."

"Enn fought on as on they flooded.
Witnessed his betrothed get gutted.
Slashed his blade, banged both his gun.
A sound of a drum and the scum were gone."

"Merchants in numbers, crossing the night
Spotted the officer in his fight
And rode to his aid to join the affray
The savages then simply melted away."

"Proof! With Enn and his lost bride
That the scourge of the land was but a tribe.
A monstrous tribe of killers, skilled
But brutes who bled and could be killed!"

"The captain rode to Holyrood.
Inside the palace in somber mood
Sought an audience with the King
And told him of the odious sting."

"The King was throned with Anne the Dane
And he well knew of witches bane
For limping to the Firth of Forth
'The Gideon' hit from a storm boiled north."

"His childish bride implied black magic.
Swore she spied a cursed pelagic.
Back in Denmark repercussions
Found a slew of Satan's covens."

"Scotland also women burned.
The massed trials was where he'd learned
Of sorcery, his expertise
To write 'The Demonologies."

"The Samson hag had howled a scorcher.
Confessed a verse whilst under torture,
That Satan's foe upon this earth
Was James 6th and soon the 1st."

"And so the King his ear was keen
To hear of tell of Sawney Bean.
Requested his Castalien band

'Compose me ditties of the damned."

"Cast as hero in the title,
Routing evil by the bible.
A fictitious righteous homicidal
He checked the text for signs of libel."

"My story stirred him up a storm
To arm his army in the morn.
Commanded Enn to navigate
To where he'd come eradicate."

"His Highness led the holy force
Four hundred men and forty horse.
Sniffer dogs to sniff the rot,
Four cannon and some cannon shot
And gunpowder to blow their plot."

"A friend's was Enn as we trekked the glen
Solace in our loss.
But we were not wiser men
As we thought they troops of moss."

"Some sung songs stomping the prairie
To calm the King when he got wary
Harassed from a past kidnap
He asked his cortège-
'Falter back"

"The coast was hunt to Bannane head
Till dusk had set without a thread.
Then a musky scent of dead

Was scented by a sniffer hound.
The fiendish cave was finally found."

"Six abreast with fixed bayonets
We marched into a mire.
Shadow things gleamed harrowed scenes
Born of brandished fire."

"Nerves were spent as dreams were bent
In purple circled gaze
Flambeaux sticks played demon tricks
On the walls of the garbled maze."

"James who was by far a fool
Halted by a sunken pool
And thus defended by the fosse
Said –
 'Strum minstrels! Before the cross."

"And as they stayed and played and prayed
I, Enn and skittish men
Marched to fetid maw.
A crab brigade held us at bay
For they had raised claw."

"To reeking ink we flinching inched

When a rat gang scampered, rabid.
Shooted caps swarmed storms of bats
And warned that we'd invaded."

"The stifled quiet after rifles fired
Cracked the cavity.
Then eyes got burned as we turned and
learned
Of wracked depravity."

"We bumped about in sickened blunder,
Sick in mind and sick with chunder.
Our souls were so torn asunder
In the charnel pit of people plunder."

"Seven stacks of salted corpses!
Baskets of torsos, main courses.
Soup tureens of human beings
Nibbled ears in pickle jars
Eyeballs in an ornate vase.
A store of sawn off gnawed on arses!"

"Seared in morbid awe we stood
A soldier leaked a lake of blood
Panic stricken torches fell
Then another's fatal yell."

"Rushed on the Goth! With a rage of wroth
And chaos cleaved the ranks
A hatchet heaving crazed behemoth
Hewed a swathe in our flanks."

"She led a hate filled hurricane
A heinous typhoon.
It slammed into our barricades
And ploughed through the platoon."

"Nine men died. Four more would die
More knelt for mercy's pity
Thence came a clear rung battle cry
Which shored us up with gritty"

"Pro Rege Et Lege!
Defend the liege!'
Aroused the rousing shout.
The captain broke the siege to bend
The battle from a rout."

"Kindled privates raised to rally
Muskets spat a leaden volley.
Vengeful swords pricked many more.
Enn ripped on –

'The King! The law!'
Till all that was defiant
The mammoth axe wield matriarch
And her mirrored triad giant."

"Sacrilege! None shall pass!
Defile his snooze-ed church!'

The mothers trine lurched to sign
A necro oozing mass."

"Hails of slugs drilled four fat thugs
But on they fought on, praying.
Swung sword and axe till shells collapsed
Emptied with the spraying."

"Gunpowder booms saw sulphur fumes
Form layered waves of brume.
A shadow loomed in hazed gloom
Smoked out his basest tomb."

"The grog soaked ogre, half hungover
Eyed his empires fall.
Dead or caught the air was fraught
As he prowled with a dual maul."

"But ire was in the eye of Enn.
His spouse assassin now he ken!
His passion grew to fired glow
He steeled to pounce.
To smite his foe."

"Sawney's daunting presence failed.
Crumbled, paled. He tumbled, nailed.
His glowered glare blurred to stoned.
The bully beat. Chained and owned."

"Unclean fiend!
James preened behind a wall of armed ward.
His clique of poets notebooks primed
For histories record.

"Force it kneel. May fierce it feel
The justice of our Lord!
Your souls to pay on judgement day.
Today you'll bless your King.
You'll beg me grace for this disgrace
So yield! And kiss my ring!"

"The ogre bridled. Dangled guards.
Strode towards, spoke with barbs.
Fettered, held and half blind drunk

Still scared the King and sucked his spunk."

"Kneeling? Yielding? Kissing rings?
No more talk of witless things!
For we both Kings and sires of mice
And are we not both mired in vice?"

"I reap souls and rape a few.
Are souls also thy own taboo?
I seen so, seen your mincing crew!
There is a difference twixt us two…
Your fret of me! Not I of you!"

"Twas at that moment from the pool
Infants from a horror school
Clamped his padded pants like leeches.
The King released and soiled his breeches."

"He screamed a stream of cussing words,
The likes of which I'd never heard

"A cussed towel!"

"His bowel the lighter.
More an author than a fighter."

"As biting brats were beaten back
The Kings façade began to crack.
What before a cod piece itch
Exploded as a nervous glitch."

"He dropped his rood to rabbit bounce
Howled in bandy legged flounce.
Howls of haunts of headless mums
And cussed repents of sodding sons."

"Sawney and his hellish brood
Smirked in relish at the lewd
Eccentric monarch on display.
James, ashamed, vowed they would pay."

"Forty seven cannibals lugged out to
mornings light
They mocked him locked in manacles,
Jeered on in wounded plight."

"Jeering all the march duration
Acting the Kings defamation
 Ornery taunting flaunting bilboes
In the swamps betwixt the enclose
Of Tollbooth's incarceration
James citing rightful divination

And to avoid his abdication
Ordered a mass mutilation."

"From the raucous throng were ripped
Their glottis tongues and dogs were tipped.
A slippy slope thence I slipped."

"The family thrown in an oubliette.
My stance seen as a sovereign threat.
My expulsion from the August members.
A week which saw my words as embers."

"Censors raided publish places
Papers pulped or burnt to ashes
Cinders made of any cases
Of literature containing traces.
Any hint of this affair
Written or whispered would ensnare."

"Back on the street out the Jacobean elite
Poor pay packets pending.
He pledged my course
'The tower or worse!
 If you write again offending!"

"The Judge was Gruesome.

The charge high treason.
No defence. Not a voice could reason.
Yanked by ox to Leith's port market.
The men folk chained to form an orbit."

"The women watched atop their pyres
As Bean stalks wrenched off with pliers.
They added to the mound of meat
With severed hands and severed feet."

"Sawney was the last expire.
Stomped bloodied stumps
In a tongueless blare.
They waited till his ire was quenched.
Then they fired three pyres
Of whis weans and wenches."

"The screams of weans bore a burden hard.
Worse was the sound as my books were charred.
The cheers of the crowd soon tired and died
As the fire bit weans were the last Beans fried."

"Silence settled on the square.
Their ashes sailed to snow the air.

A lone crow stared his murderous stare.
Then a warning to attending there
From Crown control a proclamation –

"To tattlers – trial and compensation!
To any who speak of this they'd seen.
To the tattered quiet compensation.
Those at a loss 'cause of Sawney Bean."

Book 3
The Tale of the Ruined Hume and Bean

Thomas-
"So I stand pinched but yet can clinch
A trump of a scoop to gloat
For your priest revealed
That the son that you shield
Is His! - Which he sold for a groat."

"A crazed male cattle gored your old mans tackle,
His Bulls did'nae spore his wife.

I've a tale to grip the rabble
It'll claw back my flawed life"

"A best seller read! Half demon brood
And half the seed of the cloth!
Your son is star in my book bizarre
Saga of the church and the goth."

"And I want you know as its time to go
Bend the bows of your tree
That every Bean sowed and the bane that
they bowed
Will end with this story!"

Agnes-
"I was a slave in a vampires cave!
I'm a victim, as is thee.
If you've a heart you'll not impart
My boys identity.
Tear up your text and spare his neck
Print you'll snare an innocent!
End your revenge insistence!
Persevere and this I'll swear
I'll hex your short existence!"

Narrator-

It took two guards to tie her arms
Another to smother her voice
Took another two to secure the lasso
Together they heaved the hoist.

Creaked the branch that hung the minx
That clawed the hemp for air.
Not one dared glimpse her bulged glare
For fear fall foul of her jinx.

Agnes-

"No! 'Tis wrong. He's the golden one!
Let his future flourish.
A living hell will follow on,
I'll bet, if he's to perish!"

Narrator-

She tried to twist to lock the look
To deal the debt of Thomas.
To her choked despair he offed his stare
Her threat became a promise."

Agnes-

"Spirit of scourge! I command
A summons please of thee!
With thy black hand disease the land

In his vicinity!"

Narrator-
The stoked curse invoked a storm,
A deluge on the downcast morn.
Rain clouds were darkened further more
By crows with 'Murder!' in their caw.

She wailed in sway till she went grey
Limp fell her tiny fists.
The town folk say that to this day
Her grieving ghost persists.

As Agnes' demise pronounced
A courier cantered in, announced
'Bess is dead! Long live the queen!'
And folk forgot the hanging Bean.

The menace loomed as was presumed
From the Stuart regime
Soon Alba swept for secrets kept,
To keep his image clean.

A hasty London migrate
The theatre thrill an aim.
Disguised he merged with compromised

Falsified new name.

Thus part crusade of the puppet parade
Who came to curry favour
In Southwark's sinful suburb stayed
To soak the stimulus flavour.

Some happy weeks in cloistered streets
He sauntered to inspire.
Too distract to ink of the vibe and the stink
He planned a moons retire.

A month's long hibernation
With supplies to feed his need.
Sat scribbling expositions
For thespians to read.

Huddled in a hovel on the saga that he
planned
Thomas at his novel noticed not the noxious
land.
Alighted at his writing desk he'd only quit to
sleep
Did not notice pestilence had galloped in to
reap.

The manuscript completed he emerged to
copper sun
Then dropped the print in shock and squint
Saw what had thus become.
He strayed dismayed to theatre town
The start his souls decay-
The playhouses were closed down…
The plague had come to play.

In squat distraught by the padlocked wrought
Iron gates of The Globe
Reflecting at his luckless lot
His conscience self in probe.

And as he analysing
For answers this states
A threat bade up him rising
Up face to face his fate.

"A boy to rent? A city gent?
Lodging in my manor!"
A cutlass pressed and ego dent
By the muggers manner.

Arrested in penury, pondering this strife
Up surged a misted fury

Which flipped the threatened knife.
When the mist had melted and tempest had
becalmed
An anxious ringing riled him
As regard the vagabond.

The sound was but tinnitus stress
Assumed a watch mans whistle.
He braced escape the stepped recess
And perforated gristle.

He paused to pluck the robbers purse,
The white noise was decreased
So stopped surveyed Agnes' curse
Saw what she had released…

This pulsing place that now was raw
A crucifix on every door
The grass that grew where trundled carts
As merchants moved to further parts.
No artistes left to grace the arts
Save painters with a raft of red
To cross the spot where dwelled the dead.

The damaged pimps with famished whores
As punters sniffed the bubo sores.

Unmanaged pits with silent cheers
Mere memories of the bitten bears
And fighting cocks with un-bet claws.

Prophetically, a leak of laughter
The promised pox had carved disaster.
Swept through sewers, cellars, rafters
It squeezed the dogs and sneezed the masters
Panicked the preachings of the pastors.

Oily rats as slick as foxes
Breakfasted in rancid boxes
Boxes full of blackened corpses
Stacked by those whose hacking coughing
Would soon fill a stacking coffin.

This hub of industry derailed
As ailing London's heartbeat failed.
Still the city stink prevailed…

In desolate delirium he reeled in disbelief
Then sought a whore emporium to dicker
some relief.

"Pray enter!" Bade the brothels ma'am
"Drink to our decline!"

For the prostitutes had looted
A polluted shop of wine.

Pickled in a drunken trance
To part forget, to part enhance
The tickled perfumed tender first
Female touch that purged his purse.

He swigged in swing his quart of ale
Spurting to her fickle wail
Bangs not heard as spurt on time
The hammered nails of quarantine.

Shut up in dark without a meal
Fumbling, finding things by feel
Feeling kegs but needing bread
Felt the rigor mortis dead.

Caged in the contaminated boudoir!
Crazed in a claustrophobic stupor
As fevered tarts with oozing marks
Farted as he starved.

He drank to numb what he'd become.
His buggered life in tatters.
Muggers blood in sleep he swum

Of which he still bespattered.

One by one in shuttered gloom
The dying doxies raved their doom.
One by one the pleasure rooms
Came to be contagious tombs.

His rasping harlots final rantings
Played imaginations feared.
With this last call girl departing
Horrific mirages appeared.

His stomach stewed in bile and beer
In addled altered stance,
Famine straddled him to jeer
Joined Mort and Pestilence.

Three awful figures in cavort
Ruminated an abort,
To yearn the germ to end his life
For he had not crutch of child or wife.
And he had no pride just waves of shame.
Hunger plundered him insane.

Cradling his fading maid
In faint hallucination

Saw the brothel Sawney's cave
With Sawney in ovation.

A salivating fantasy
Thoughts he fought to plug
Sawney hailed him family
Applauded bloody stub.

Kaleidoscopes of woe and hope,
Groped knockers, black in taint.
A mocking demon tempted tope
'Abstain!'
Yelled shoulder Saint."

Refreshed!
With budding breast of Jezebel
And emptied jugs of ale
He feasted on infected Belle
Where ecstasy prevailed.

Sated with the tepid tit
He closed red eyes of rheum
Then froze he stiff in terror fit
As Sawney filled the room.

"Bore more, my heir. To reap your prize!

This feasts initiation.
Take heart, arise! For I will share
My kingdom of damnation!"

And it was odd to hear this laud
As tongueless his dictation.

Then his hanging father, with opposing slant
Harangued him hanging opposite
A rope rasping the rant

"Adopted by the cannibal?
A savage sod I've groomed!
Your foster father forced thy
Soul forever doomed.
For Eve you've eat urgo upset
Omniscient God!"

Giant triplets manoeuvred
Embraced their sibling quad.

Powerless in sodden sheets
To shake the freakish dream
Gertrude Bean held piquant teats
And filled his mouth with cream.

Gagging on the pungent milk
A further fail to waken bilk
With carrion mother showering guilt
Harrying with –
"It's all your fault!"

In his hazed dreamscape jungle
Her assault saw Thomas crumble.
The baked Bean bairns hoorayed their uncle.

Victims that he never knew
Lined up torment him in a queue.
Stiff soldiers sang in symphony
Conducted by sir Timothy.

The philharmonic force of eaten
Sought to be some sort of beacon
To sway step sisters incest lusts,
Thrusting lice infested tufts.

Two armies faced each other
On psychotic plains.
An eroticising coma
As the virus coursed his veins.

A horny flame haired Sawney

And the Devils feral pack
Fought fantastic in their fury
In the fray as prey fought back.

The quarry in the orgy
As decayed as zombie fiend
Sang frisky songs of glory
Of revenge on Sawney Bean.

Four horsemen of apocalypse
All gathered now and three
Galloped round the battlefield
Round War, the referee.

Twelve nights were like twelve lifetimes
With every second Hell.
Two weeks, too weak to turn his cheek
To block his beak the smell.

A fighting, biting, fornicating
Fortnight 'midst the mass.
Bubonic brass the audience
In scenes see Bosch aghast.

Paralysed in excrement,
But that what shat him most…

Malevolence personified
In Her passion powered ghost.

Searchers scouring back end alleys
Tasked to find blighted bodies.
The bagnio reached to sanitise
When they heard inside his haunted cries.

Tearing boards of the bordello doors
They found him fitting on the floor.
He bit the grabbing hands of creatures.
The searchers had Agnes' features.

Bound atop the body truck
His clouting arms tight tied
Gagged with rags of bedding, dragged
To an Alms house. Dumped outside.

Spanning all of Autumn,
He raved the winters husk.
His burden London Sodom
He disbousomed dawn till dusk.

And no escape in slumber
When return to Sawney's cave.

An involuntary spelunker
In the bunkers of his brain.

"It's all your fault!'
The sick all cried
'It's all his fault!'
Before they died.
Grim miasma's of discord
As the reaper scythed an empty ward.

They tried in vain assuage his pain
But was a thankless task
For what he saw the nurses wore
A cursing Agnes mask.

And when they tried to soothe with words
Spoken soft in poise
All he ever heard was a
Spiteful poisoned noise.

And when they tried massage his skin
Silk fingers stroked his limbs.
All he ever felt was ten
Scratching steel pins.

Till winters thaw a laboured chore

His mentality infernal.
The malady rid 'twas their main bid
The infirmary back to normal.

Spring released the nurses ceased
Indulge his lunacy
His nightshirt seized and six girls heaved
Him out to a jubilee.

There the gentle poet
Who'd been pushed to a pariah
Partook with passing plethora
Who were praising a messiah
What he thought he caused to morph
Into a Gomorrah
Turned to be a polished place
With a gala aura.

With flowers strung above the mews
And flags. And food on barbecues.
The crowds enthusing on the march
Pressed sips of wine to lips of parch
They swept him to a towered arch.

Addled for an actor in antic attire
Up he raised onto the dais

With toga togged choir.
Seldom felt him welcome
So his spirits soared
As the Roman actors welcomed him aboard.

The reverberating rostrum was in bosting
beat
Thomas full of frolic now in design to greet
The object of their ardour
Perhap' replenish emptied zeal
The performers splayed in grovel,
Horizontal, to reveal
A perfect panorama
With the plebeians prostrate.
The procession was a picture
Progressing to the gate.

But noticing their focus and he shattered like
a glass,
Unleashing floods of venom
At the sight of such a farce.

A pretentious farce as plastic
As this plaster arch constructed
For he that so corrupted
That he persecuted persons

Having parallel persuasions.

He! Producer of the righteous read
That castigating bigots creed.
Authorising executions
Of Samuels semblancing Susan's
Whilst practising the very acts
To contradict his gospel 'facts'.

For hailing in a fancy carriage
Hamming. Fronting a sham marriage.
He who aved the peasantry
As if from Caesars pedigree
Was James the poof who sat aloof
With offspring ringed
To guise his gayness
To resemble two faced Janus.

The play was all a fallacy
For a fraud and Pharisee.

The charade that passed the podium
Was stared in utter odium.
In disgust that flushed his looks
At the burner of his books
At the censor of his words

At the fawn of moron herds
Fallen posing in revere
Brown nosing for the premier
This premier with prim veneer
Who'd fucked him,
Then fucked his career.
Slew all but silent sycophants.
A psycho since he shat his pants.

He erupted off the pulpit
To the car, to scar the culprit.

The slobbering monarch wept in horror
Seeping piss and voiding honour
Pegged his possessed paramour,
Petrified at what he saw.

His ex-pet swearing vendetta
Roaring 'Rape!'
To souse him wetter.
Citing crimes, the blood been spilled
Of the witness flood he'd killed.
For the shower of lovers spurned
For all the cowering women burned.
For the poets pride forsaken.
For his art and arse he'd taken.

James to save his oily skin
Hid beneath his infant kin.
He shielded under Charles his son
As it shouted 'Charlatan!'

Forward fanned four Agnes clones
Who floored the tramp
And broke his bones.
On the orders of Lord Enn
Who saw him not, a former friend
But his onus eyesores cleanse
So threw the anus in the Thames.

Inhaling lungs of sucking slime
Was much a blessed release
For with the pain the poltergeists
Appearances had ceased.

Even comprehending that his bane
Was James the Queen
His mark of expiration was
The hark of Agnes Bean.

Part 2

Book 4
Dimmock's Yellow Diary

Humfrey-
'Twas almost May, the weather gay,
In London on 'The Lion'
Cowards some. Some slipped away,
In slipped the Devils scion.

One twenty tonnes with twenty guns
Raised by Raleigh's purse.
Sails unfurled to the new world.
'The Lion' shipped the curse.

The settlers cheered, 'The Lion' veered
Into the estuary
They'd left their lives to sink or strive

A distant colony.
Sink or strive. Die or survive
We headed out to sea.

We aimed toward America
A strange land I didn't know
They prayed, the companies clerica
But still a storm did blow.

The boat it rocked, from left to right
Just later in that week
We had not passed the Isle of Wight,
I lost my joyous streak.

A hurricane to drain my vim.
We bounced like barrelled balls.
None could hold their stomachs in
In spiteful Satan squalls.

Spit and spew washed the decks
As doubt drenched every mind
White thought-
 'What Warlock placed a hex?'
As England left behind.

The Devils spawn spurned the storm

Like acid in a potion.
We were flimsy fodder for
The fuming spume shot ocean.

Euphoria was emptied.
With nerves set all a quiver
We a tiny matchstick on
An endless friendless river.

I seasick and I homesick,
A fortnight from our shores.
The ship it start to stink of shit
When passed the green Azores.

In amidst of all the thunder
Off strayed a sister sloop
But the pilot yearned for plunder
Refusing to regroup.

He ignored the Governor's orders,
Belittled Whites displeasure
His sailors were all hoarders
Of plundered Spanish treasure.

The flyboat lost and still we tossed,
Dry peas waxed in a rattle.

And still he'd root about for loot
And treated us like cattle.

I vocalised the verdant lies
Of Raleigh's promised paradise.
Salt spray stung my scoured eyes,
I gormandised by parasites.

The lice, the lies, the nauseous sap,
I hankered for my home.
I hankered back, reverse the map
Reverse this reckless roam.

When it becalmed the boredom bit,
In doldrums on the brine
The buccaneering foreign git
We nicknamed now 'the swine.'

As tedium set I soon beget
To find out things to know.
'Twixt the pilot and the scion
I wished a storm to blow.

I wished a wind to wash them off
But 'twas a balmy breeze
I wished it wild to take the child,

Wash off the Portuguese.
I wished a gale to break the jail
To free me on the seas.

As if in jail, the ambience
Was a steaming kettle
'Twas the buck that pushed his luck
To try to test the mettle
Of swabs against the settlers.
Slurred those who'd set to settle.

He'd whisper lies, antagonise
Both sides, from stern to bow
He'd fucking thrive on raucous tides
And relish every row.

Fights with fists and arguments,
Pioneers, marines.
The men incensed, in their defence
'Twas smears and smoke screens.

Sussed by the assistant Howe
Who sussed the source of strife
Howe banished him remain below
For slandering the wives.

They put him down, that Billy Brown
To bunk amongst the men
To help the cook, but by his look
I'd swear he less than ten.

Less than ten down from the Glen
A Scot in tongue and hair.
Swampy eyes held hate and lies
Stilled fear with sullen stare.

The cook, a pirate, Johnnie Bright
Known for thuggery
Had lost and now was fret to fight
Bill in the scullery.

For weeks he'd piss into the dish,
Slops had rat bones found
He'd grin and spit and say it fish
That beastly Billy Brown
Then raise his fists and all would wish
He buried in the ground.

And it was only Governor White
A good man, friend and boss
Insisted on his life's respite
Stopped to the deep sea toss.

It was the Governors luckless word
That staid their hands to kill
They should've flipped him overboard
To save them all from Bill.

They could have lived in calm accord
And all be thriving still.
If they'd have thrown him overboard
And saved themselves from Bill.

Puritan prudes still heard the lewd
Accounts of acts obscene.
Said stories rude to stoke the feud
'Twixt husbands and marines.

Scandal! The damage dealt.
The tension trailing he.
Howe and help they whipped a welt
Right to the Carribbea'.
They whipped a welt in Williams pelt,
Were blind to escapees.

Two Irish ran. They saw the signs
When dropped at last our anchor.
The bailing slime were papist swines

That added to our rancour.

It came to light that both they might
Both Catholic and bigot.
Both had rode before with White
Could guide a Spanish frigate.

With the thought of being caught
Or of mutiny
Fernandez fraught and so he sought
To keep us out at sea.

But land! Oh blessed be the Lord!
Like rats we ran and then we poured
The sand to scrub the months of grime
And for a time our spirits soured
To feel our feet upon the ground.
And beer was cheered and passed around.

I sat upon sweet terra firma
Whilst scented breezes softly murmured.
For there a time the pining's yield
To see again an English field
And smell again a summer meadow
Or hark again a homily echo.
To fear not a fraught tomorrow.

So sat we under balmy palms
To sun ourselves and be becalmed.
A pilgrim preached a placid psalm...

Twas not long fore things went wrong
Again by witchery
Gathered fruit seared every throat,
Scorched in misery.

What island Sprite had we upset?
Were it the hold held ghoul?
Unslaked our burning throats with wet
Fire from a pool.

Flaming throats from poisoned ponds
Threats from those who chose abscond
An unsticking of our glue
From the hostile harried crew.
Sickness on the ship of woe
We sailed again to slick unknown.

Those taut weeks the tempers frayed.
To the Spics we were betrayed
Arms were readied for a raid.
The greedy pilot sought to stray

From our pre planned destinations
To rob the gold off Spanish galleons.

The swine's sole aim was for a groat
His itch outshone the mission
From dawn to dusk he tore the throat
Of White's triumphant vision.

They cussed it was each other's fault.
He would not stop the ship for salt.
In the cloying awesome hot
The stinking food it start to rot.

Rot set in the crew aboard,
Fernandez formed the foe
I faced the foe that chased the hoard
Than face the thing below.

The thing below was maddened now
His lunacy was ripe
He rippled in his hate for Howe
Whipped to a wicked gripe.

And on and on and on our way
In undulating fields of grey
Slumped and sour and getting sicker

Sick of constant grinding bicker.

The sun it beat upon our necks
Beat us down to sprawl the decks
I fade but faced its foreign fire
Than shade to face the orphans ire.

So slumped and sick and hot and hungry
I riddled through with doleful doubt
In wane, the furnace fogged me dumbly
To not defy the profane lout.

And then a shout of 'Land Ahoy!
Oh how we thumped our backs with joy.
All old rifts were healing over
We cheered as if the cliffs of Dover.

It was a good and godly sight
The first my glimpse upon the might-y
'Merica, our task to master.
The pastors prayed us from disaster.

My heart in flutter with the honour.
Proud to represent the Crown.
A rush to rowboats on thrown ropes,
The sailors helped to swing us down.

We rowed onto the Roanoke
We blessed. We chosen few
Exalt as every oar stroke
Propelled toward a noble coup.

Twas faraway from Chesapeake Bay
But ranked our happiest times
We beached the craft then walked our way
Through many mystique pines.

The scent of pines, exciting times
We stumbled on the fort…
Nought but that that spoke of crimes
That caused this posts abort.

Dwellings all vacated,
Cinders signalled torching
I felt a wraiths stirred hatred
That spelt an omen warning.

Where were the men of earlier?
Where Francis Drake's slaves?
The mystery was murkier
Than the encircled waves.

We whittled all the woods around
For signs of Grenville's men
But little there and little found
And little did we ken.

Little did we ken but we
Safe and sound ashore
We'd conquered the Atlantic sea,
Which filled with dogged valour.

We'd conquered and we'd bought the Lord
To where the Lord was not
We claimed it by his righteous sword
And hallowed first this plot.

A vote was cast, we'd stay a while
Convert this spot to Zion
We'd stay upon this arcane isle
And scorn the stinking 'Lion'.

'The Lion' that felt like the pit
With tempers running raw.
A bastard piloting the ship,
A fiend locked in the store.

But here we were as men reborn

In lands that we felt free
Trees were felled and logs were sawn
In England's colony.
Plans were drawn for babies born
To grow this new country
Though fingers torn to plant the corn
For rain we did not see.

A man feels much a greater man
If artisan is he
Souls were fed by tools in hands,
Erect for family.

The sun shone on our faces,
God shone in the breast
We habituated places
That God had placed to test.

And we were gay, contented
As we worked the day like mules.
We believed we heaven sent-ed
As we toiled with our tools.

At night, the sky awash with stars
White told of past narratives
By firelight he'd paint the sight

Of fights and friendly natives.

He'd draw exotic pictures
Of the Red man's size and girth.
We pure quoted scriptures.
Both sides blessed the birth
Of Eleanor - his daughters-
The countries Christian first.

Some say they saw a future fate
Forged in the flaming embers
This land, the Crown's, we'd consecrate
By our committed members.

A miracle! The flyboat sailed!
On Spicer's navigation.
God was praised and Jesus hailed
We jumped with jubilation!

Our companions thus united!
In a fortified bubble.
We planned Manteo knighted
Negate the native trouble.

With muskets and with pointed stakes
Felt safe within, secure

We'd shoot the deer and fish the lakes
With faith we would endure.

But still no drops for soil to slake
Dropped from the clear azure.
No rain to rake for crops to take
Though prayed for by us pure.

We evolved it to a Protestant town
Assembled in high humour.
Then a shout of 'Where is Howe?'
We rushed around the rumour.

We rushed to search and called and climbed
Treetops for forty acres
We prodded bush, our pistols primed
Hilltops to bluffs and breakers.

Poor George Howe was found some how
Bought back atop a barrow
His scalp was mashed, his body slashed
And porcupined with arrows.

His pin covered figure, disfigured by Wicca
Was a mesh of whip cut welts.
Rusty strands clenched in raw hands

I'd swear were the strands of the Celt's.

Oh the panic that befell the camp!
A blizzard bit, devoid of damp
I knew but dared not say aloud-
The cyclone struck without a cloud.
Panic hit the crowd some more
By clouds of crows with 'Kill' in caw.

No more a place of innocence,
Tranquility was broke.
Vendetta fuelled militants
Scoured the Roanoke.

In John White fell a red mist
He bayed for the blood of the brutes.
In his hapless luck and temper twist
They maimed Manteo's troops.

And now no Indian ally
And I foresaw much much worse
And I fret to stay and dally
But to scuttle from the curse.

Ah! The terrors when I shut my lids!
The horrors haunting me

I saw the murders of the kids
I craved a boisterous sea.

I begged be off, be to the Bay
But 'twas a big conundrum
As Billy Brown was in the way
More dread than what I'd run from.

We buried Howe in a shallow shrine
As the dirt was heat baked dust
Belatedly White saw the sign
And signalled a move was a must.

"No!" Said the swine, leant o'er the bow
"This is where thou'll keep!"
"How" said I "is the state of the boy?"
-"Why, I put him ashore last week!"

White roared the defraud of the declared debt
Then ordered the row to the fort.
I sobbed and begged to the sun had set,
Offered vast awards for transport.

I paid him much a whole years wage
Of a merchant in the city
Whilst in my ears there rang the rage

Of the departing committee.

I foot a fine to the eager swine
To bunk in John White's quarters.
And I spelt the sign that it past the time
To leave these malignant waters.

A rabid rook of Roanoke
Flew round to mocketh me
The goading rook and a boding smoke
Imprisoned me at sea.

The bastard crow with its bastard caw!
It's caws was gross and ribald!
It seared my mind so I sealed my door
With pages from my bible.

I care'th not, not a raindrop fell,
Or of Virginia's christening
For we'd ushered in a living hell,
Lured God away from listening.

I saw well enough from my sealed room.
Saw White in his desperation,
Saw the colonies impending doom
Prophesied from my hibernation.

The cursed crow came till I went insane
To squawk along my sill
I ill with pain as it squawked the name
Of the nemesis name of Bill.

John White pleaded every day
'A passage - to replenish stocks!'
And every day the swine said "Nay!
You'll stay here on these rocks!"

I urged speed off for we'd woke the wroth
Of some ungodly djinn.
We'd caused a chasm by the anti Adam.
Took evil to Eden to sin.

Oh dear Lord, let this nightmare cease!
I implore you Christ almighty.
I'll pray all day the demise of the beast
If you'd grease the path to Blighty.

An answering nor'easter gale
Drove us from the cursed coast.
The Lion sailed as my prayers prevailed
Upon the Holy Ghost.

Ye Gods, we bobbed about like corks
But all my prayers and all my thoughts
Went to repatriating English ports,
To escape the toxic pirate fort
And sail away from stinking tenures.
The swine talked still of stealing ventures.

The weather calmed and faired to nicer.
The flyboat neared with Edward Spicer.
I clocked to the noble captains right
Proud on the prow stood Governor White.

Bless be Spicer! Bless his eyes
For taking White to get supplies,
Spicer exposed his unwound neck
To let the Governor board his decks.

I spied White's hex at work again
When the capstan broke, the men in pain.
His friendship I began to rue
To see the captains crippled crew.
The crew with broken bones and worse
Care of White and his ebony curse.

Half a crew, no wind blew
Both boats were lagged in loiters.

Lazy, for the spirits knew-
Chastisement for exploiters.

We went from utter idleness
To wild and wet wer-storms
Most sagged in sickened lifelessness
Like dolls in human forms.

Like men morphed into mannequins,
Pus coughed from corrupt lungs.
Like the strangled cut from scaffoldings
With scurvy bloodied gums.

And I could barely hold my quill
These terror'd months returning
For the ghost crow sat upon my sill
And stated I'd be burning.

And still the swine swept the seas,
Sniffing round for spoils.
Scorned his shipmates with disease,
The swabs with swollen boils.

With ailing cries the undead scratched
For weeks upon my door.
Morbid magpies sought my stash

Till sighted Blighty's shore.

And men were dead and more were dread
To find some similar fates
And White had fled when Spicer said
He'd lost near half his mates.

I went to bed when I hit my stead
Once passed the city gates.
I sought my bed though through my head
Foreboding fluctuates.

I stayed in bed or prayed in church
And bathed in holy water.
Bed or church sat on a perch
The ghost crow sat in squawker.

Haunt me not, devil bird!
Thou with the glower of Bill.
With thy auburn hair and sadists stare
Sat there on my sill.

Be gone! And come back never more!
You rub me raw with your cursing caw
Your eyes of moss and cinnamon mane.
I wish ye gone! Ye phantom bane!

No cajoling, no reward
Could see me back again on board
Nor Raleigh's title guaranties
For chance to meet Mephistopheles.

The Painter White was pinched in pain
And daily got more frantic
The war with Spain had squashed his aim
To cross a quick Atlantic.

By and by, over and over and over yet
White to return did try
But Britain lost all interest,
Found fatter fish to fry…

Cold dread sweats here in my bed.
I petrified at stuff crow said
Solidified from toe to head
As a statue cast in lead.

In dreams we be an ant colony
Tortured by a Titan
A fiend from Greek mythology,
An age this vision frightened.

-Bills head, no ears but wings instead
Trampled by his giant tread
And everywhere we hid Bill sees us
Replacing his with the viz of Jesus.
Bicey eyes were stone and starey
My antenna'd eyes forever wary
I see him flapping, fornicating Mary!

How to halt rapes of the Virgin
Whilst my sanity was blurring?

Heaven weeping whilst I sleeping
Imagining the ghastly reaping,
The harvesting and then the eating
Of the souls that we'd forsaken
By the freak that we had taken…

Oh blasphemy! Oh heresy!
These acts I see are haunting me!
I wish him dead across the sea
To perish and to set me free.

Oh Lord what had we gone and done?
I'd burn for bringing Satan's son
I fret. But return for my redemption?
I need survive, top up my pension.

Then Liz –Beth called, to serve the war
The rich could pay. She'd arm the poor.
And still the ghost crow at my door
Squawked hateful sounds. More and more.

More and more his murderous caw
From months to years outside my door
Louder now than he before.
Foul demon from the days of yore.

Too rich. No wish to join the militia.
I'd fight not Parma's army.
A Spanish pike could'na prick my psych
Like a petrifying journey.

So I paid most of my pension
To stay at home, flat broke.
Twisting at night in tension
About the Roanoke.

I twisted, nor no business.
No income from my stores.
And I damned to hell as witness
The desecration of those foreign shores.

With Philips Armada firmly beat,
Ships released from off the fleet.
Who should come upon my street?
He with planned out expedition.
White rose me from my chamber prison.

I rose composed a holy quest
Rose for my financier.
A sainthood waited – I to be blessed
When slayed the necromancer.

We sailed in spring in 'The Hopewell'
The name was apt for White.
My spirit soared as parallel
Sailed Spicer in 'Moonlight''

A fortune Raleigh had now paid-
To impress the heir of Boleyn.
I sought return to crusade.
White to see his kin.

Three. Fraught. Years.
Shear panic, shedding tears.
Pacing, pleading, every day got harder.
The missing leader. Father. Grandfather.
Refused return to stock their larder.

The stress was mighty on his health.
A shadow of his former self.
Coughing, sniffing, limping, aching.
His heart three years of straining, breaking.
Bright eyed again as we were making
Waves to weigh with fresher hope.
Wending back to Roanoke.

The return was mild. The weather fairer.
'Cept detours for our ships to plunder.
I was wired to right our error
White was gripped in hopeful wonder.

Gripped in hopeful wonder,
But he anxious and irate.
For the Pirates pursued plunder
And White could hardly wait.
His people all? Or torn asunder?
Keen to find out what their fate.

And then we spied a plume of smoke!
Two rowboats rowed to Roanoke
And Edward led, who on top form
Saw he not the sudden storm.

Catastrophe! What alchemy
Had mixed this evil gale?
We yelled to turn the tragedy.
Yelled to no avail.

The sea was as a living snake
In wreathing, writhing twist.
It coiled and dipped and in its wake
There sprayed a blinding mist.

A cloaking blinding mist, I wist
It enveloped in its covers.
Revealed when neared much as I feared
Drowned Spicer and six others.

As Spicer shown his sodden grave
I sagged in sickened swound.
I wished it White in swallowed wave,
For'd tarnished those around.

White pressed proceed and Cocke agreed,
Time not for terse bereaving.
To land at noon, to flute the tune
'Greensleeves.' Perhap' receiving .

More merry English tunes were struck,

Tempt those with nerves a seared.
But White again was out of luck
For not a soul appeared.

Nor not a soul came to the shore
For cannons echoed blast
So walked we did to where before
Three years before had past.

We walked the old familiar way,
No man dared speak a word
For dank and dismal felt the day.
The fort. Sat a blackbird.

The settlement forsaken,
The dwellings were dismantled.
White screamed in desperation
And all of us stood rankled.

"Where art thee girls? Where did ye go?
Lord pity on the pious!"
There shadowed him a spectral....
CROw, "where AT!- Oh AnaNais?"

What was this sign carved on a pine?
This cryptic code of CRO?

Bedamn my beard for that blackbird
It cruel appeared to know.

It locked on me its callous eyes.
I startled in its sight
It conjured blustered bruising skies
To drain me of my fight.

I drained of every inch of fight-
Bled from the feathered phantom.
I fled in throttled fearful flight
To the 'Hopewell's' sanctum.

The clouds were crows with boiling wings
And thunder rolls cawed hateful things.
The wind whipped rigging sang a song
As we dipped and crashed and bobbed along.
'Greensleeves' the cables crooked tune.
Ghastly green I fell in swoon.

Miles, sweet miles when I awoke
Relief! As miles from Roanoke.
We skated still on sea churned foam
But sweet Lord we headed home.

The men pressed home, or mutiny.

It shattered John White's soul.
He slumped in distressed scrutiny,
Spent by squandered goal.

Shattered as so near, so far.
He'd die a broken wreck.
I'll sit at home with my memoirs
To save my snakebit neck.

Tis the Devil and the deep blue sea
That keeps me in my gown
I'll venture not for any fee.
Not leave my London Town.

I'll pray and stay here in my cot.
Pray God would shoot his bolt!
Pray He lightning strikes the rot,
Forgives the missions fault.

Pray away my weakness
Pray the evil we'd accessed
Did'na strew a blanket bleakness
On that virgin country west.

Book 5
Matwau Rising

Narrator-
Hanging from the hairy tree
That she herself did plant
The folk they took no notice
Of the wretches wretched rant.

The memory of wee Agnes
In Girvan was always vague,
Not one recalled the first one
Of the witch that called the plague.

No one recalled her first boy.
Her sibling and her son
Who had the Sawney spinach eye.
Not The Fathers greyish one.

For Agnes was expectant
When escaped from Sawney's lair.

Had had her fathers giant child
With ginger giant hair.

The babe was big, quadruple
And a spit for Sawney's hue
And so berserk and brutal
That she'd hidden him from view.

Six years she'd hidden William
Who was then more twice her size
Then packed him off to London
With her purse and in disguise.

Her ploughman paid four seamen
To take him out to sea
To sail away the demon
On a ship to set her free.

A decade that she'd lived in dread,
A returning Billy riled.
Ten recovered, then she'd said
"I'll have another child"

A decade gone and Sawney done
They'd hauled the menace down.
She'd cherished on her sandy son

And hoped the ginger drowned.
She hoped him dead her giant red
Horror Billy Brown.

1589-
Summer

Tom Smart-
"Now Governor Dare,
Let us be clear
In sane and sober eye.
If we stay here it is our fear
That we will surely die"

"We're out of powder, low on chowder
Chained to try to farm,
You pious have your wives to ride.
We have Madam Palm"

"For two full years we tried to rear,
But blisters, boils and bunions
And backs a bent enough to tear
A bag o' bloody onions."

"Our backs all hurt through constant work
From toiling in the heat.

And though you might have fun at night
We landed hand or seat"

"And while you pray and make the hay
We missing, one a month!
If we stay we're premier prey,
Packaged for the hunt."

"We're frontline as we work the field
No ammo. Aching balls.
You grind behind your wooden shield
Of pointy pine tree walls"

"We have no shot and woe begot
Those stranded on their own.
Frustration felt as we in melt
To till this dusty loam."

"I sussed the game, frustrate Spain's aim
"By loading here with thugs...
It's lack of Dames and rain for grain.
We're bursting! Drained like mugs."

"You zealots have your girls or God,
And think We lewd and dirty.
But we think abstinence is odd

Agreed all of us thirty."

"Us thirty are to live like they.
How nature had intended!
We'll root as in the Native way,
With Manteo's wenches"

"We choose to crude - not civil,
To naked, nay attire.
We'll be fulfilled and serve until
Returns the bloody liar."

"Where is the bloody liar White?
Where has your law pa gone?
'S' not what we signed, this life of shite
Procured it by a con"

"We bought here on a promise!
Now we shadowed with White's hex.
We been gullible and novice
And denied the fairer sex"

"This bloody drought and us without
No dainty one to hold.
This lands severe, unless your queer
And not a sniff o' gold."

"The lack of skin to kiss, caress
We cannot work or focus!
For we are men and we possess
Throbbing red hot pokers…"

Ananias Dare-
"Civility! Calm ye your vibe!
Upon this council meet!
Those who choose Manteo's tribe
I pray you have a seat"

"I pray ye quickly find the Christ
Or be ye unprotected!
Leave the fold and pay the price
Ye devil lust infected."

"Manteo'll hold you in low esteem
At best you'll be his slaves.
Be celibate! And drop your dream
Of rutting savage maids."

"Be celibate! And celebrate
Good hard honest toil.
Then you'll enter heavens gate!
Reward for staying loyal."

"You'll have your fun- with angels
After you have died!
Unbolt celestial stables
For what you've been denied."

"Just hold on till your life is gone,
Forget all earthly pleasures!
Your muscle pains are for sweet gains
To take cherubic treasures."

"If we divide we halve our force.
I'll tell thee Smart the gob.
If leave the fort you'll set your course
To ruin by your knob.
Hold your horse and be the source-
An inspiring modern Job..."

Winter.

Ananias and Eleanor-
"We're down to forty fighting men
Since all the rest have split.
But lo, we have no sex pests left,
To God the best submit."

"I fear him! Ananias dear
I spy him 'yond the trees!
I see his carni-vorous stare
It fears my blood to freeze."

"We must pray harder Eleanor!
Invite the Holy Ghost.
The spirits shy as secular
Sods still at this post."

"I fear him for he floods my dreams
I'm owned. I am his goods!
I fear the red. Fear he's not dead
And watching from the woods.
I fear he tread toward my bed
To claim me as his goods."

"We'll construct a wooden church!
And That will cure our woe.
The Lord will sight from cloudy perch
And gifts he will bestow!"

"I dread him, Ananias Dare.
In sleep He presses close.
His fingers fondle me down there,
He haunts this heathen post."

"Tis 'cause of unbelievers!
The cause of all this fuss,
The famine and the fevers.
He's turned his back on us!"

"I don't believe he's dead, Dare
From snippets that I've heard.
I hear him in my nightmare
Shape shifting to a bird"

"We'll spend more time in praising,
Worship is the cure.
By His grace amazing
We'll survive this epic tour"

"I'm ravaged by a rancid Rook
Who rapes me every night!
It is the savage Scottish cook
Transforming after flight."

"Be calm Eleanor. Calm ye may
Upon this Christmas eve
Profane ye not on Gods day,
Your safe if you believe!"

"A hideous ginger jackdaw
I'm afraid! Too weak to fight.
He consumes me! I'm a ruined whore
Succumbing to his might."

"Sleep my dear. Virginia's there.
You'll wake her with your raves!
Be not afraid, this palisade
'S for repulsing brutal braves."

"I spied his eyes along our trip.
A sexual pervert!
Staring off my blouse and slip,
Thinking off my skirt!"

"No more Eleanor, with that thought
You'll tempt Old Nick to hear.
We're safe, us three, within this fort
I pray you lose your fear…"

Narrator-
Upon the Ships arrival
Bill packed himself a pack
To insure for his survival,
Stole cheeses off the rack.

The sailors trussed him in a skiff,
Marooned him on the beach.
Skilfully he scaled the cliff
Planned lessons he'd to teach.

The heir felt not a twinge of fear
Amongst the watchful trees.
Was not alone as crows had flown
When whiffed the moulding cheese.

There he sat and bonded
With multi fowl disciples.
Sat and fed and pondered
Revenge on all his rivals.

There he founded, crow surrounded
By warriors of Wanchese
Who revered him on the spot as some
God from overseas.

He was bought onto their warlock
Who had prophesied the word-
A flame haired one of spirit stock
Who had mastered the black bird.

The witch doctor – Sugnog
Sycophantically purred
A glorifying dialogue,
Extolled the coppered bird.

They sat him on a palanquin
Dressed in feathered cloak.
Worshipped by the Algonquin
Around the Roanoke.

They hailed him as a ray of sun,
With halo of red hair.
The murder always followed on
For crumbs of dairies share.

He made the most of all the praise,
Lapping all the licking.
Prophesied the end of days.
The raptures clock was ticking.

The chief that went to London
Did not need too much persuading.
The sun child quoth 'It hath begun!
With start of White's invading.'

Said White men 'They the demon scum!

They've come to take the land!
If you'll arm and give me some
I'll make a holy stand!"

Bill hand picked a jihadi band.
He picked the most suspicious.
Most religious mostly and
The bloody mostly vicious.

Those obeyed the things he said.
Those cruel with bovine nature,
Those who needed to be led,
Those who'd bolst his stature.

He orchestrated Howe's attack,
The ambush on the river.
One brave, Chogan, held him back
From eating out Howe's liver.

That night a squaw, in anguished yaw,
Staggering and shrieky
Screamed a mortifying roar-
Of murder in her teepee.

Chogan's scalp had fateful flap
His head was almost severed.

No eyes, crow claws stuffed in the gap.
Slack mouth was stuffed with feathers.

No trial, nor any summoning,
For Sugnog staid their hands.
For he'd foretold the coming
Of red thunder in their lands.

He foretold but fearful worried
And did not know what to do
For the sun child was now sullied
For he'd broke the tribes taboo.

Taboos were broke and oft' was stoke
The fires of holy battle.
Victory foretold in smoke.
Heathens were as chattel.

One a week they'd stalk and slay
Settlers, other clans.
His gang obliged in angst obey
To aid his predator plans.

They soon knew what he doing
When he dragged the meat away.
For soon his crew were chewing

Off the flesh from off their prey.

Sugnog saw of his mistake
And voiced it to the cowed-
That their prophet was a fake...
They found him disembowelled.

He went to squat the shamans hut
And fostered all the hype.
Carrion crows kept up the guise,
Their wage was human tripe.

Step by step he sought to climb,
Further up the tower.
Now a rung below the prime.
He had the shamans power.

And while the crops were withered,
Most the tribe it start to starve.
He acknowledged as a wizard
For he'd conjured meat to carve.

His holy gang of slayers
Weren't the only players fed.
Soothsayers in compliance
Could too feed upon his dead.

Sated Mystics spread the myth-
His blood deeds came to lore.
His enterprise excessive with
A mass of pain and gore.

And all the time he authorised-
'It sanctified and right!
These meals are merely infidels
For our appetite!'

A sickness swept o'er the tribe,
The flux it cut them down.
Those survived were those subscribed
To the will o' Billy Brown.

They thought him More a prophet Lord,
Their belly's he kept filling.
Their pox was cured when he procured
Cheese dosed with penicillin.

The doubters lay like skeletons-
Famished, ulcered, thin.
His band of rogues had healthy tones
With glowing golden skin.

They glowed in only outer shell
Inside they more, more beast.
As like the crows that sought the smell,
More savage every feast.

Wanchese lost more his grip,
Too weak to weald his lever.
No cheese to cure did pass his lip
When struck with yellow fever.

And in a lavish ceremony,
Kuffars round them ailing
'Matwau' –mortal enemy-
The messiah named at naming.

Matwau! Spoke in fearful awe
By menaced unbelievers.
Echoed by the murders caw
To taunt those struck with fevers.

Matwau turned his twenty team
To live a year nomadic.
Pursued his dream of his regime,
Now hunting here sporadic.

So they crossed unto to the mainland

To conquer, in canoes
To wrought an utter wasteland
To rape, to kill, abuse.

They terrorised the native stock,
Subdued with terrorism.
Expanded his expanding flock
By bowed evangelism.

They found a camp of negroes
And slaughtered all but three.
The three with savage egos
Who joined the company.

And in recruit from other tribes.
Those sloughed in decadence.
Chose Indians with vicious vibes,
Some seven Secotans.

Six settlers too who'd evil view.
Each with a villain story.
Who'd fled the fort to join the crew
Led by Charlie Flory.

Thirty seven men at arms,
Marauders. Matwau leading.

Terrorising native farms.
Ten squaws were farmed for breeding.

Terrorising other tribes
Who praised or paid a tax.
To stay alive they paid a bribe
Or suffered ghastly acts.

On their return with Matwau grown
As big as any brave
With high desire to take the throne,
To show the chief his grave.

Wanchese was fading, dying
But he still held off his homage.
His deity denying
Held the healing stale fromage.

Near Yuletide and with smatter'd snow,
The chieftain a la mort.
Chief Matwau had designs to go
Attack the settlers fort.

He painted all his warriors red,
Their faces Corvus black
To fill the foe of freeze, of dread

In the night attack.

The cannibals swarmed the silent grove.
Midnight, Christmas Eve
They stunned and beat and roped and drove
The pilgrims to the sea.

Matwau's attack supremely timed.
They streamed the stockades pass.
No settler had a weapon primed,
As posed in praise en masse.

The screams were sweet off of the meat,
Music from the larder.
Matwau stiff for he could sniff
Sheer terror for his ardour.

His ardour quenched by sordid vice
As settlers scattered round like mice.
His clan bayed at his raping rage,
Bayed at buggered Tony Cage.
Cage that bared his crucifix,
Ripped to bits by lunatics.

And it was a hellish sight
The things he did to him that night.

In sick religious ritual..
Hailed as dripped in visceral.
As he hailed for killing, rutting
Someone desperate was woodcutting.

No weapon primed but carved a sign,
Tom Stevens on a tree
To hope to show this strike that Crow-
Was bought about by He.

Caught off guard at Christmas,
Every settler bound.
Sculling past the isthmus,
O'er the Pamlico sound.
The beatings but a litmus
Test from he who newly crowned.

Part 3

Book 6
The Fears of Eleanor Dare

Eleanor and Ananias-
"Please smother dear Virginia,
Ananias, grant me that.
Before It takes, begins the
Render of her fat.
Roped I cannot end her!
Ananias! Grant me that!"

"Before It boils and eats her
Let us have a last embrace.
I'll tell her that I love her.
And I'd love to take her place"

"We've failed and now let's end her
For I cannot stand her hurt.
Now! I fear I will incur
The wrath of that pervert!"

"Eleanor have faith again,
Escaped some of us, seven.
And if we cannot get away
I'll see thee both in heaven."

"White will come a smiting-
Restore the symmetry.
Disinfect he all the blighting.
On return with infantry."

"I cannot, Ananais Dare
And will not share your faith!
If less in grovel, more aware
We'd more of us be safe!"

"Faith's not helped, has bought us harm!
I wish you'd change your tack!
Matwau's eaten half your arm!
You pray God grows it back??"

"I'm drained, my wife. Faith quenches fear.

My life is almost spent.
I'm sorry to have bought you here
Sorry you'll not repent."

"I hope there be an after life!
For there I'll make amends
Hope you lose your fear, my wife
And prayer pays dividends."

"Oh I fearful Ananais!
 I'd prefer if I were food.
And keep your useless prayers
For I'm raped to boost Its brood.
It's peeling back my layers
Till I'm crushed and coarse and crude."

Eleanor-
"And now your gone, my husband!
My darling daughter too.
It sautéed with your pious blood and
Made Virginia stew."

"My darling little daughter!
I swear I'll make It pay!
I'll debt settle for your slaughter.

Going to gut the grim gourmet."

"Marge Harvey shown no mercy,
Devoured with Dyonis.
With death she was too fussy.
She slipped in her abyss!"

"Always moving, moves away
This caravan of woe.
Not three nights we stop and stay
Then on our way to go."

"In blazing sun or squelching snow
In pain and injury
Dragged through the sleet with bleeding feet.
Each move a misery."

"Gasping, parched, we forced to march,
The ground in summer scorch.
It put to torch the towns It crossed
That would not swing around."

"We marched through spikes of winter frost.
And more collapsed and more were lost.
I watch them fall and eaten raw,
Watched them raked by rancid claw.

Watched dead bodies turn and toss
As crows inside jostled, thrust
To dine on jam below the crust."

"They snatch, It's zealous cronies,
To offer, on a skewer.
It blessed at sickened ceremonies
For meat that It procured."

"It blessed and praised and sits upraised
On Its throne of bones.
They chant and dance around It crazed,
Dance around the towns they razed
Intoning to the doomed ones groans"

"Skins are tanned for wigwams,
It makes me scrub the skulls.
Now I ache, tied to a stake
As now I'm on parole.
For this mistake of tried escape
It hammers every hole."

"I've stitched a human mantle-
I'm so cold, tied to a hitch.
It binds me by my ankle
And treats me as Its bitch."

"Always on, always West,
A waters winding track.
To where we stop, to where It blessed
By the Procoughtronack."

"Here they made It welcome.
Here they're similar kinds.
It'll turn their town to bedlam
For It soaks absorbent minds."

"Lo! And so, not one year on
To see what It inflicted!
It fuels all fervent men in fawn,
Perfervid elevated.
Forces strong to weak feed on,
Fuels entire family porn!
To see it so and still they go
And hold It venerated?"

"To see them all still worship It?
Its back tracked them primeval.
Their village turned a hellish pit
Since Its 'divine' arrival."

"Season melts to seasons,

Melt to diabolic years.
Matwau with his legions
Itch to spread Its holy fears."

"So we away, spread more Its seed,
For Matwau's sexual sating.
For more to breed, for It decreed
A menu change for mating."

"Each day my thoughts are suicide!
But I'll press on, be strong.
As all but eight of us have died
And one needs right the wrong."

"Now goes Lizzie Viccars,
Rosie, Emmie Merrimoth.
Defiled by queues of rippers
Raped and stripped, tipped in the broth."

"The four last children cuddle close,
Shaken by each scream.
As each taken by the Crow
It tears my very seam."

"Lord forgive! Those timid kids!
I corse with liquid pain.

Squealing sounds as slaughtered pigs.
Their yells drill in my brain."

"I must keep calm and quiet
To survive this Armageddon.
Complicit and compliant
Mind and soul I'll seek to deaden."

"It made me eat the flesh of men!
On pain of being shredded!
I'm as a beast kept in a pen
I've fell. Twas what I've dreaded!"

"Ananias! Ye of little lumen!
I need help to stay my sense
To help me stay a human.
I need help with my defence!
Help me ride this sick offence.
Ease my tension, my suspense
In Its pressured presence
Help regain my draining essence!"

"Defend me Ananias, and soothe my sanity.
Your presence is but just a glimpse
Of strength and sympathy."

"We've stopped our roams as nomads.
Found this cavern. Now Its lair.
I fear Its ginger gonads,
Please sustain me, Ani Dare!"

"You who but a shadow
But my only consolation.
You wisp as smoke tobacco.
Scant relief from rapine Raven."

"You shimmered haze on cavern wall
Who dances with the lantern.
You I miss above them all
You who only can turn
My funk and awe for what's in store…"

"Its day is Monday-Moonday.
Where they kneel for Its advice.
To the rising moon they fawn and pray
Then gut a sacrifice."

"It dictates Its deeds on human skin!
That skin is consecrated..
They task Its sagas in a spin,
It's deeds exaggerated."

"It's word is spread through fearful skies!
Its 'miracles' are basic lies.
None dare differ, fear reprisals.
Still more revere the wing-ed idol."

"I fear the crescent, pumpkin moon,
Fear noon and dusk and dawn
It magnified as I ballooned
With Matwau's bastard spawn."

"I hate it! Hate this foreign thing!
That grows inside of me!
Know it spawn of the Crow King,
Collapsed humanity.

"Just I survived. I, no other.
I who lives in chains.
Matwau said I'd suffer
So much more than labor pains
If I kill the clone of mother,
Ordered Agnes be her name."

"It ordered me, dead husband!
To bear Its child a she!
If not got what It customed
It come chow down on me!"

"I fearist now my fathers dead.
I dreamt him in the nether.
It bound. I cannot cave my head-
Unite us all together."

"The Chesapeake, I think I know
The placing of this cave.
I'll scratch another hint in stone
For soldiery to save."

"I'll carve in rocks more clues for
Justice be delivered.
Incriminating Matwau-
The woe that cunt hath triggered."

"It is a she! And I survive!
Although I do not live.
This babe might save. For her I'll drive
On. And love I'll give."

"And now she born and I forlorn
To think the thoughts I had
Though she his, she is adored,
My antidote to sad."

"She just a little parcel,
She knows not this be wrong
To munch the metatarsal
Of a squaw it'd once belong."

"I fearful of her future,
Of her ferocious sire
Fear I'll not long can suture
Of It's debased desire."

"But it seems she is the prized.
Heads all other runts.
Not too much that she chastised
For disrespectful stunts."

"I will not be Its factory!
Though cherish I this tot.
I've damaged what's inside of me
And sterilised my twat."

"I'll civilise she that's mine,
And shun Its other brood
Won't add another to the nine.
A solitary feud."

"I will not fall compliant

Like the other mothers seem.
I'd die with my defiance
Than expand Its horror team."

"Now Agnes six, exploring
Though I tie her in the crèche
As the caverns sights abhorring,
I disguise the human flesh."

"She plays with bones as if they're dolls
An innocence heart breaking.
I shield her from what It involves
Me in and my degrading."

"I shield her from Its followers
Who skulk about the cave
The fiends who are the swallowers
Of sermons most depraved."

"I tell her all the screams are songs
Of spirits who've released.
Soothe her as these hateful wrongs
Seem only to increase."

"Now a little older, a lot harder to protect.
Matwau calls her mamma

And she's interest to his sect.
I got some dead for what I said-
Sliced from arse to ear!
Three warriors who approached her bed.
Dead, when went too near."

"Mamma! The giant constant calls
A girl who's age is nine.
Repulsed! My skin doth crawl!
It's crossed the bottom line"

"I'll kill It if I get the chance.
If conquer can my quiver.
I'll stab if not in terror trance
And give it to the giver"

"But Lord I am so frightened
And I fear I'd miss the goal.
Please make me more enlightened
How to end the giant troll."

"When It nears I shudder, shaking.
 I'm so useless when I'm riled
But Its murder plans I'm making
To protect my feral child."

"She's to survive if I'm to drive
In It a yard of steel.
The cult will kill and then we will
Be but another meal."

"So help me God or thee my spouse
Oh Ananias, hear?
Help me with the succubus louse
When right the time is near."

"Tis the slightest compensation
When It disappears for days
But I'm guarded by Its Ravens
Who do all that It obeys."

"They sit and guard the entrance
And watch with much malaise.
They watch with all resemblance
Of dun Devils in their gaze."

"I fear them, demon avians!
Fear my girl they'll get
Black hearted little aliens,
The monsters evil pets."

"Way they strut to guard the brothel.

Way they root in people offal.
Pickings dripping off their beak.
The sounds they make as if they speak."

"Whore!Whore!' The chorus caws
'Whore!' Cave echoed chimes.
'Why for I is?' I asks them this.
'This!' Repeats the mimes."

"Can I go on much further?
With this murder, bloody murder!
My life gets only harsher
As I've lost now all my armour.
I'm in constant blood and filth!
But I'll not just die a martyr
I've this testimony to spilth.
And I'll not be dead and rested
Till I have the beast arrested."

"And these streams of screaming victims
From a multitude of tribes
Are stuffed into the pigpens
Then they snuffed. I tan their hides."

"I tan their skin but from within
I pray their souls to glide.

I pray for they to find a way
The peace they've been denied."

"The murder agitated!
The clan have run for cover.
Six assassinated!
It felt the death of mother!"

"Oh Ananias please protect,
It wrenched Ness to Its lair!
Tis a first I see It wept
When It wept into her hair."

"It is so fearful sickening
To see It slumped and slobbering.
The atmosphere is thickening
The menace growing, hovering
Its odour overpowering!
And now Its eyes are glowering
About for a devouring!
Can't spit, my spittle's souring.
I'm so anxious with alarm!"

"Still It calls her mamma-
I fear It do her harm!
 I twisted with the trauma

At Its mummy nursing drama!
Slim hope It's killed by Karma.
So her chance is with her charm."

"I thank ye spirit intervention!
But I'm shaken to the core.
I know of Its intention
If Agnes blossoms more.
I torn apart in tension
Predicting what's in store."

"I've got to get her out of here
Pay loads for her escape.
I'll approach the Buccaneer
To try to stop her rape."

"An, I so miss Miss Virginy
But I do love little Agnes.
I'll bribe Bright by a Guinea
Renew his pirate practise"

"I've promised John a fortune
To secure Ness a release.
Enough to buy his Whore Town
If he'd ship her overseas."

"Johnny Bright was set alight
His treachery uncovered.
His torched remains were torn by kite
And rat and crab and buzzard."

"An English boat was seen to float
Into Chesapeake bay.
Matwau slit five English throats
And scared the ship away."

"In agonising torture
Bright spilled his guts and told.
Matwau sent a searcher,
For he flushed with thoughts of gold."

"Oh dark despair! I shot with woe,
So close was a reprieve.
I'd packed a sack for Ness to go
And told her time to leave."

"It made me watch the sinking mast
Down o'er the horizon.
With that ship all hope had passed.
My soul it start to siphon."

"It sucked me of my marrow

Till I could not draw a breath.
Agnes stopped Its arrow
To halt my wished for death."

"She threw her body over mine
And challenged Matwau's will.
Her tiny frame had paused designs
Of Its lust to kill."

"She thought she'd done a favour!
My save from gallows rope.
But now I seek my saviour
For I've lost all of my hope."

"Yet years go by I still deny
The primate I've become.
Your ghost is now what I rely
Lest I be dull and dumb."

"I rely on you, dead husband
As Agnes disappears.
I don't know what she does and
It fills me full of fears.
I try but now I cannot stand.
I fear my ending nears."

"My sleep disturbed by hard-core haunts,
Now Agnes is pubescent.
I fear It of Its obscene wants,
Motives of pure putrescence."

"I fear Its going to fuck her.
Like It tries to fuck her mind
I'm out of tricks to deter-
It. I still am chained, confined."

"Ananias' apparition-
I see ye in my head.
Please be more than just a vision
And send spirits from the dead!"

"Summon ghosts to liquidate!
Time ticks for teenage Agnes!
Tell fathers ghost participate-
To crush the cannibal Canis!"

"Fifteen years!
I've cried a sea of hopeless tears.
Fostering my phobic fears,
Forced to every degradation
I beg you for my one salvation,
Save Agnes from this aberration."

"I offer I as sacrifice!
Oh spirits listen, please!
Save her from Its monstrous vice.
Oh ghosts! Oh God!
My life for she's.
I've so much fear...
Oh please, God.
Please…"

Book 7
Wahunusanocock

Narrator-
Jamestown camp was ravaged,
Frozen. Running out of food.
Ransacking's by the savages
Had cast a bitter mood.

Its leaders ordered Smith explore.
To seek out native allies.

To trade or raid to top their store
Before the townships demise.

In a vast and frosty wasteland
Up the Chickahominy
He surrounded by a war band
Of two hundred Pamunkey.

They yanked him out an icy marsh.
Marched miles of barren plateaux.
Through woods, streams and waist high grass
To Werowocomoco.

Throughout the town he dragged around
With whoops of gloat and glory.
To the longhouse, bound, to sit astound-id
By the sovereigns story.

Chief Powhatan-
"Captain Smith, I'll tell you if
Protect you Pocohontos.
For He was one. If others come
Disaster be upon us."

"My daughter saved your pale neck.
Suspect so for a reason.

So go retell the saga back.
I confide in your liaison.
So harken!
For with this, I've saved the life of you
For you to tell all Jamestown
The things I had to do…"

"He bought the woe to Roanoke
To taint tribes of the naked.
Bought disease, disgust, despair,
Convincing he was sacred."

"I'd never ever seen His like
Like His corrupted sin,
Like feasting on the flesh of men
Or laying with your kin."

"Like mating with the dying,
Then used the fucked for broth.
Drank tears the doomed were crying
To fuel ferocious wroth."

"He Atasaya incarnate.
Was uglier than Okee.
He murdered, mauled and maimed and ate
The Potomac to Pamunkey."

"Men were bowed and taken in,
Saw Him son of kizis.
He rose to tribal shaman,
Warped Wanchese' wishes."

"He turned the anglophilic chief
To hate your little isle.
Replaced his faith with disbelief
His loyalty with bile."

"He stoked a bilious hatred,
Which caused Wanchese to croak.
With the chieftainship vacated
He ruled the Roanoke."

"He ruled them and he schooled them
And He drained them of their force.
His maxim was in mayhem
As He steered them all off course."

"He distorted deity spirits.
He sickened weak men's souls.
He pressed me to my limits
By pushing forth his goals."

"Now you may say I'm savage
For I dealt a heavy hand,
But white hands came to ravage
When you landed in my land."

"At first you made me to believe
That you came here to trade.
It's in your marrow to deceive,
To rob to wreck to raid."

"You came, you burnt and then you learnt
You needed us to nourish!
You stole our corn and then you warned
Malice not to flourish."

"It's in your marrow, yet I see
All men can act as swine!
Far crueller is the one that He
Believes that He divine"

"Far crueller His fanatics!
The kind that He subverted.
The sane veered to erratics
By the word of the perverted."

"This inhumane behaviour,

Appalling acts of odd
Was sanctioned by a 'saviour'.
He saw himself a God"

"Crow God. False. Fickle. Fake
Crafty, cruel and clever.
An outer state like burnished plate.
Inside was black as feather."

"The Muslim men, the darker skinned
Left a year 'fore they
I scattered to a fairer wind
And still they thrive today."

"We met! I saw in desperate eyes
That they were wronged, deceived.
Abandoned by your English lies
 I granted their reprieve."

"So men can stay and share this land
And live a life of bliss.
If men give more than they demand.
If men take not the piss."

"If men will live in harmony
Then I will let men live!

If spread they not perversity
Forebears nay not forgive."

" Matwau came and just his name
Was black. The bite of night!
His deeds of shame spread like flame
To set our world alight."

"He came, campaigned. From Engerland
And sought sanctification.
He claimed This was His holy land.
Hallowed by His invasion."

"No bear, no wolf, no wolverine
Was Matwau's fury rival.
Migrates with his mujahideen
Caused carnage on arrival."

"Yet the butchery went unspoke
For more than fourteen summers.
For a bowdlerising cloak
Was cast to gag all utters"

"Rumours, whispers, tokens,
Finds of carcasses torn bloody.
Some tried to read the omens,

Some blamed the Pukwudgie."

"Nuttah! My heart!
Too soon, at twelve for you depart,
When life for you had barely start.
Taken by a nightmares knife!

Sad for second favourite wife!"

"Missing from the meadow
Sent to the afterlife,
I'll rejoin you as a shadow
Now vanquish-ed this strife."

"I informed soon of this issue
When found she in lagoon.
She stripped of every sinew.
Her sockets stuffed with plumes."

"I overflowed with vengefulness
To cleave the guilty head.
Demanded gathered evidence
As Nuttah nice in bed."

"Twas only with commanding
That more cases came to know.

With witnesses expanding
Their ordeals with feathered foe."

"All my priests then prophesied
That- that came crusade.
Foresaw the one that qualified,
The one that they portrayed."

"They'd read more signs in entrails.
Read eagles in their flight,
Had proved with clued credentials
The cause of all this blight."

"Foresaw potential triumph
As He bred and spread His seed.
He'd busted scores of hymens
To champion his creed."

"The sorcerers saw symptoms
As they read the stormy skies,
Foresaw barbaric kingdoms
From the seeds of emerald eyes."

"Foretold that no mere normal man
To best it would enough.
They brewed their spells to find who can-

'Twas Operchancanough!"

"My little kin a champion!
He chosen by a charm.
Amulets from Algonquian
Shamans shielded harm."

"He strong of mind and strong in arm!
Strong enough to stop the swarm.
A formidable! A bull on form.
He, they said, who's soul was white
He, they said, could fight the fight."

"Operchancanough the giant
Stood taller by a head
Than all others and reliant
To face the looming dread."

"I gathered all the gallant
From the thirty tribes of mine.
The braves with combat talent
Were to track down the malign."

"Aft' many moons my mavens,
And counsellors of war
Diagnosed the rot was Ravens,

And in order to restore
Must purge from all locations
 Matwau's scope to spore."

"My brother with four hundred
For nearly four full years
Sought out and tortured, hunted-
The copper Crow adheres.

"I did not seek negotiate
To reveal kept secret layers.
I found by modes excruciate
The cave of Atasaya."

"I hurted his devotees
Who'd like a plague had spread
Their broadening diocese,
Enlarged His range of dread."

"Smoke, Smith, my pipe of peace.
Now wash your hands in water.
Relax, recline, eat of this feast-
Hear why I gave no quarter."

"A werowance called Parahunt,
In scout for russet flock

Stumbled on a reverent,
A chief of Chowanoc."

"His spotter in a hophornbeam
Had told of seeing things-
This chief by a secluded stream
Had signed the folded wings."

"Parahunt with ninety
Attacked the Caravan
The fight they fought was mighty
And they slaughtered to a man."

"The Chowanoc's fought to final breath
Whilst sounding cawing sounds,
As if they sought a caustic death.
As if Elysium bound."

"Not one did to surrender-
The followers of the wing.
As slayed sang they the splendour
Of their tawny cannibal King."

"Still more reports were filtering
Of doctrine spread around.
An orthodoxy simmering

In a Tuscarora town."

"Operchancanough, the chief, the bear
With forty mounted horses
In seeking finding Matwau's lair
Pillaged with his forces"

"It was a blazing blood soaked dusk,
Felled families of fanatics.
They tore the town to smouldered husk
To purge of foul dogmatics."

"The town head man was forced confess,
The chief of Ocanhonan.
To tell from were the tendrils spread.
Then shot by forty bowmen."

"Gave Operchancanough a lead
Up the Powhatan river
They paddled miles in manic speed
For justice to deliver."

"A snaking convoy of canoes
Went west seeking man-eaters.
The wicked one was now pursued,
Loomed time for the dictator."

"Thirty strains and thirty rests
The troops at end of tether.
Some faltered in the righteous quest
-Talk was He ruled the weather."

"The thunder rolled, the rain it lashed
Till half the paddle boats were smashed.
The war band ran on feet for days
Disorientated by the haze"

"The forest lost to mist!
The wind to fearsome blow.
My brother forced insist
The men proceed to go"

"At night they huddled in clusters,
Fearful of their of foe
Wind whipped sounds in blusters,
It howled at them to go."

"He beat and screamed the men proceed,
They frigid, full of fright.
For it seemed the trees did bleed
In this realm of night."

"Bleeding trees bore people fruit
Which clattered from bare branches.
As neared the village of the brute,
Smacked by savage avalanches."

"Their blitz surprise was nullified
By screaming sentinels.
The soldiery stood stultified
By crowing decibels."

"Crows darked the skies and with their cries
They darked my armies daring.
The crying caws tipped men and squaws
To charge in ready, raring."

"They dropped from trees, out under leaves
Behind, before, about.
Surrounded my Powhatan chief
And sought to check him out."

"They circled as they growling, snarling,
Those of the aberration.
Those whose souls were twisted, gnarling,
Filtered to each generation."

"Toothless crones likes bags of bones,

Lime eyed infants lobbing stones
Squaws on fours were chanting verses
Men fat on man fat spat curses."

"Chanc snatched the crows from out the air
That tried to peck his eyes.
Saw to those encircled there
A most distressed demise."

"His solid stance gave my men the chance
To counter in attack.
All perished pained, most in a trance
The possessed Procoughtronack."

"A genocide! They skinned alive
Each man, each squaw, each leaching child.
Birds were shot, dogs got kicked-ed
This town of the damned wing addicted.
Killed them all as Crow convicted.
Killed to stop what was predicted.
As each skin was sliced and peeling
Stories of The Crow came squealing".

"The tales that we had made them sing,
Those followers of the folded wing
About their God, the Raven King

Were nauseously mind boggling...
And more we sought to find this thing.
For we went strong with loathing.

"We wiped His base and now in race
To wipe Him in his lair
We'd learned the look that was His face
Knew colour of His hair"

"Back! Back! In run, to Chesapeake Bay!
Those warriors of the sun.
The tortured told us the way.
Told my soldiers of the day-
To where the Crow was said to stay
To His shrine, where he held sway.
To wrench him limb from limb…
To seek Him in His mausoleum!"

"Night and day and through a moon
We hit with gale 'pon gale.
We searched, we blinded by monsoon
But still we did not fail."

"Now listen Smith and listen well
The closure of this tune
He'd raised it up, your Christian hell

And formed it in the dunes."

"The beach was black. Awash with crows
And tied in rows and rows and rows
The old, the young, the bare, the clothed
All screaming screams of wasted woes."
"The woe was soup that thicked the air
We could not breathe from their despair.
We shivered in the long grass there
We could not move, but morbid stare!"

"Prostrate under flags of skin
We watched a ritual begin
They came and buzzed about like bees
Touching in sick ceremonies!"

"They danced, in chant,
They touched, they torched
Till all that we could smell was scorched
Flesh and all that we could hear
Was yells and whoops and woeful fear!"

"Two hundred men! But we had more!
We watched what horror shows in store.
We saw them turn and kneel and wave
Toward the cliffs, toward a cave"

"Toward Goliath, spreading blessings
-Even taller in war bonnet
From the caves mouth flame lit settings
He preached a sermon, high on it."

"Operchancanough lay boiling-
Whilst the army lay recoiling.
Ordered iron on that hill
His war cry saw them on to battle."

"The air was thick with rain of dart
Then overcast with birds
It shout Its mouth from off the mount-
Dart proved mightier than words."

"Chanc' led the push out from the bush
And clubbed and killed
Till enough blood spilled
That beach and sea were rust.
Then he filled with hatefulness
To grind the fake to dust."

"Chanc' climbed the rocks. He saw his flock
Slaughtered down below
Lightning strikes struck heads on pikes

Saw both men's anger grow."

"The battle of the behemoths!
My brother raining blows
To finish the regime of
The hulk that spread the woe."

"He took the hits of 'Chancanough.
Took till slowed, Chanc had enough.
Then was a lions triumph roar!
He smashed my brother to the floor."

"Abukcheech, a chief of his
Rushed from the beach on seeing this.
Protect his paramount with squad,
Rushed confront the down crowned God."

"Thirteen braves!
He felled them as they rushed in waves.
Smashed their skulls with tomahawks
To build a barricade of corpse.
A barrier blocking off the cave.
Sealed in Opechancanough
For time enough to finish off."

"As my brother lost his will

As Matwau went in for the kill
As He came with raised axe
He stopped and shuddered, staggered back!"

"His eyes were glazed as if in dream.
Behind a scream, a winning scream.
From His mouth spout hot blood red.
He swung His axe and She dropped dead."

"And as He swayed with quizic frown
Opechancanough had found
A fallen spear, with which was heft
Through the injured ogres chest."

"Then again, then heft some more
Till wallowed in the Giants gore.
In and out the spear kept working.
Matwau simply stood there smirking."

"He smirked as if it were a joke.
Smirked until the spear broke.
They two stood still in silent stare.
Stood in silence in His lair."

"An age was stood as if time stopped.
His rage was passed, and then He dropped.

My brother prodded. Test He deaded.
Cursed He. Kicked He. Then beheaded."

"When he through the gruesome hack,
When Matwau's head was in the sack
He heard a snivel from the black
And to inspect he circled back."

"He paused to pick the dirty hag.
As lifeless as an emptied bag.
And with a rag he wiped the grime,
Saw the elegance of her prime."

"Saw beneath the dirt, decay
A loveliness seemed sculpt of clay.
In fade but beauty still was rife.
This woman who had saved his life."

"His life was saved, he made her a grave.
For Operchancanough beguiled.
From the cave a debt repayed,
For he saved her sobbing child."

"He saved that child then married her,
She bears his children three.
Though Matwau's blood it does transfer

We are as family."

"Her sons will rule some tribes one day-
Chiefs through the mothers line.
But schooled they in ancestral ways.
Red - but trice benign."

"A gift was took. A gift I'll give
And offer up my daughter.
May chance our two tribes would forgive
And steer from senseless slaughter."

"Cast ye gaze at Matwau's head,
At this unholy vision!
See yourself who spread the dread-
Who'd forged a fake religion."

Epilogue

Narrator-

The Royal sphincter, saggy, spent,
A score more years of pounding
Was dangerously discontent.
John Rolfe was there recounting.

He'd wed Powhatans daughter.
They'd invite to the palace
Where spoke of essential slaughter
Of the second Sawney malice.

James sat in Royal fluster.
Thought to figure who the fault.
The colonies investor -
The secular sir Walt.

Raleigh, skating on thin ice
For spurning his approaches
Was soon to pay a heady price
For subjects Rolfe was broaching.

America, Raleigh's theme
To plant the English flag.
Damned to die to dare to dream,
To introduce the fag.

The atheist antagonised,

No gold or El Dorado!
Refused to kiss or rub his thighs,
Rebuffed him with bravado.

And now in foreign places
There were seeds of James' shame.
Seed of that that caused his faeces.
Same seed with different name.

He'd just released his holy book,
Was churned with ancient pain
Vowed exterminate the look
So stopped the war with Spain.

Reappeared the dread infernal!
Yet again thought it eternal.
He alone the one anointed!
By good God himself elected.
So he pointed to his censors
Who wiped most John smiths journal
And forbade, on death, to chatter
Or write upon this matter.
Hence dismissed as all boloney
Talk of the lost, eaten colony.

James paid for agitators

In Tuscarora spies
Financed a red genocide
To wipe the emerald eyes.

Massacred the native tribes
In forests, on the beaches.
A multitude to lose their lives
Because of shitty breaches.

Crapped pants! The phoney prophesies
Powhatan was proclaiming,
Four hundred men and cannibals.
The copied case inflaming.

His flames were stoked what went on there.
That fucking flaming ginger hair!
The Chief that caught it in its lair.
He was the one! Not Powhatan!
Who stopped the devil's spread.
But as he'd soiled his pantalon
It banned from written, read.

King James 1st and Sawney's genes
Marked start of foul relations.
Initiated war machines
In Powhatan-Anglo nations.

They'd contaminated the new world.
Friends were turned to fiends.
Virginia's holocaust unfurled
By Stuart and the Beans.

Matwau was not the last one-
Madman believed messiah.
More rejects were to follow on,
Sheep will seek pariahs.

The End.

23354165R00091

Printed in Great Britain
by Amazon